To the wise and wonderful women in my life
D.C.
For Anna, with love   A.H.

Text copyright © Dawn Casey

Illustrations copyright © Amanda Hall

Original edition published in English under the title *"Babushka"* by Lion Hudson plc, Oxford, England.
Copyright © 2016 Lion Hudson

First Good Books edition, 2016

Good Books books may be purchased in bulk at special discounts for sales promotion, corporate gifts, fund-raising, or educational purposes. Special editions can also be created to specifications. For details, contact the Special Sales Department, Good Books, 307 West 36th Street, 11th Floor, New York, NY 10018 or info@ skyhorsepublishing.com.

Good Books is an imprint of Skyhorse Publishing, Inc.®, a Delaware corporation.

Visit our website at www.goodbooks.com.

10 9 8 7 6 5 4 3 2 1

Library of Congress Cataloging-in-Publication Data is available on file.

Cover design by Lion Hudson plc

Cover illustration credit Amanda Hall

Print ISBN: 978-1-68099-188-8

Printed in Malaysia

Babushka

A CHRISTMAS TALE

Retold by Dawn Casey
Illustrated by Amanda Hall

Good Books®

Batavia Public Library
Batavia, Illinois

Long ago and far away, there lived a little old woman called Babushka.

Babushka was always busy. She was forever scrubbing and sweeping, washing and wiping, dusting and polishing. Her little house was as neat as a pin.

One winter's evening, when the snow lay thick upon the ground, the clouds parted and a bright star shone.

Inside, Babushka was busy polishing. She saw only the dirt and smudges on her candlesticks.

Outside, there came the sound of voices: calls, whispers, gasps of delight.

Inside, Babushka was busy sweeping. She heard only the *swish swish swish* of her own broom.

KNOCK! KNOCK! KNOCK! Even Babushka couldn't miss that.
There in the doorway stood three men, richly dressed in silk
and velvet.

"May we come in and rest awhile?" asked the travelers.
"We have journeyed far, and we are cold and hungry."

"Come in, come in!" said Babushka. "Come, warm yourselves
by the fire. Only, please, do wipe your feet."

While the travelers rested,
Babushka bustled about.
She peeled and chopped and stirred.
She cooked up a great pot of steaming
soup.
And as they ate, they talked.

"Where are you going?" Babushka asked.
"We saw a star shining in the East."
"We are following the star to the
place where a babe is born."
"A newborn child."

Babushka was quiet then, thinking of her own
children, all grown and gone, and of her
grandchildren, who lived so far away.
"Who is the child?" Babushka asked.
"A newborn king."
"The Prince of Peace."
"The Light of Love."

When the travelers were warm and well fed, they began pulling on
their boots. "We must go now, Babushka," they said, "to take gifts to
the Child. Come. Come with us."

"What," said Babushka, "without washing the dishes?"

So the travelers thanked Babushka for her kindness and rode out into the night. And Babushka stayed at home.

Babushka swept up the breadcrumbs and wiped up the soup spills. She washed the dishes. And she went to bed.

That night Babushka had a dream. She dreamed of soft hay and gentle breath; a mother's warm arms and quiet smile. She dreamed of a baby, with eyes dark and bright as the starry night.

Babushka woke to see starlight streaming through her window.

And pulling her shawl around her shoulders, she went out into the silent night. There was the star. Shining.

Babushka looked up at the star. The star looked down at Babushka.

Then her cat came and wound itself around her boots; Babushka realized how cold her toes were, and she came back inside. "I will go and find the Child," she said to herself. "And I will bring him gifts. Tomorrow…"

And, in the morning, she opened an old chest. It was full of toys. Babushka had made them all, for she loved to work with her hands. There were toys of wood, carved and painted bright. Toys of wool, knitted and stitched and sewn. They had never been played with.

Babushka filled her basket with gifts and with good things to eat: rosy apples, sweet nuts, and spicy gingerbread.
    And, pulling her shawl close around her shoulders, she set off into a morning framed with frost.

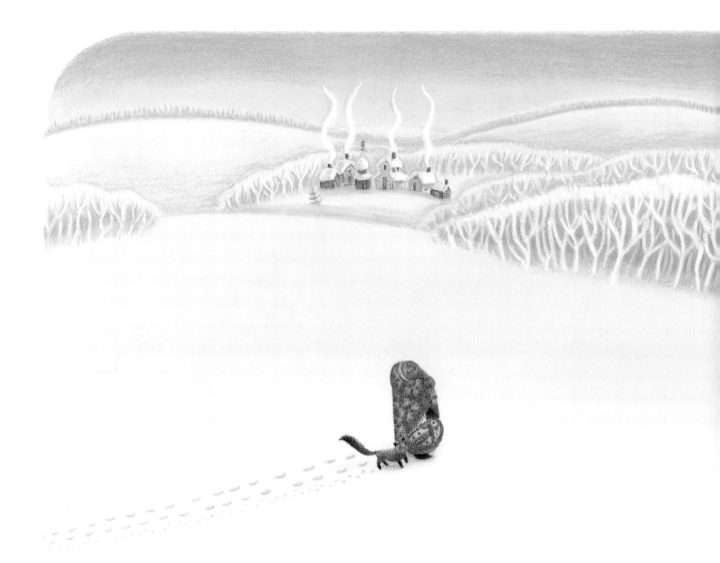

Babushka looked down for the footprints of the travelers, but the snow had covered their tracks. Babushka looked up for the star to guide her, but the morning sky was empty.

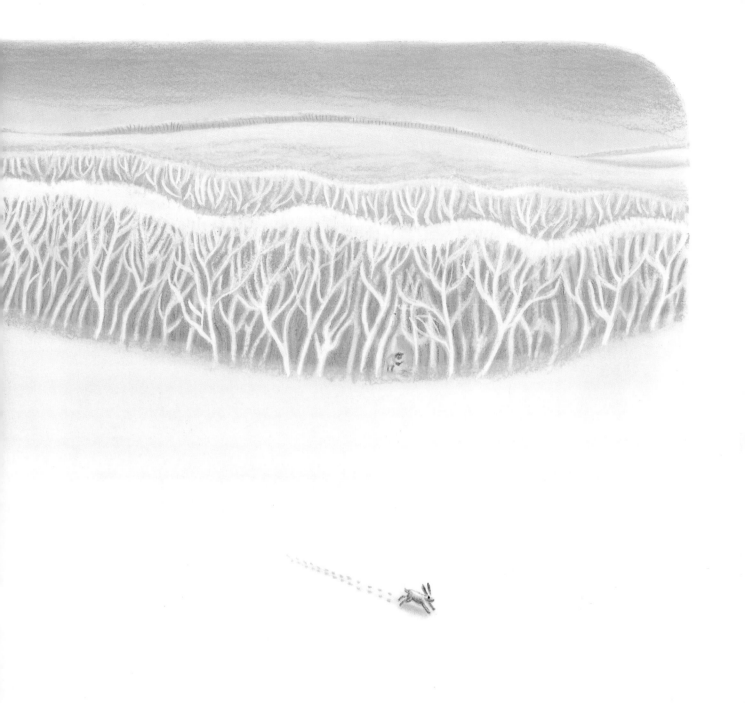

Babushka stood all alone in the cold. She didn't know
which way to go.

But for the first time in a long time, Babushka wasn't busy, she wasn't bustling. She was simply still. So she heard the sound of someone else nearby. At the edge of the forest, a girl was out gathering firewood. She was wearing such a thin dress. She was shivering with cold.

"Here, my child," said Babushka. And she took from her basket a warm knitted shawl and wrapped it around the girl's shoulders.

The girl flung her arms around Babushka and hugged her tight. Babushka laughed. And even though her toes were cold, she felt warm inside.

Babushka walked and walked. She walked until the sun set behind the winter trees. She walked until the moon rose above the silver birches.

At the frozen river, by a hole in the ice, a boy was packing away his fishing net. Babushka smiled. "Catch anything?"

The boy shook his head, and Babushka heard his tummy rumble.

"Here, my child," said Babushka. And she took from her basket a thick slice of gingerbread.

The boy bit into the gingerbread, and his eyes shone.

Babushka walked and walked. She met girls and boys with no toys to play with. So she took from her basket a doll, a whistle, a ball…

Babushka kept on walking and walking, and found children all over the land.

Babushka is still journeying. And everywhere she goes, she gives a gift. Her basket is full, and her heart is light.

Her heart is shining with the Light of Love, like a bright star in midwinter.